First Little Readers™

Stone Stew

by Liza Charlesworth

ISBN: 978-1-338-29792-8

Illustrated by Tammie Lyon

First printing, June 2018.

Hi! I am Ug.
I am hungry.
But all I have is a stone.

I know what to do!
I make a fire.

I put the stone in a pot.
Now, I will make stone stew!

"What are you making?" asks Mub.
"Stone stew," I say.
"Put in your potatoes,
and I will share it with you."

"Okay," says Mub.
She puts the potatoes
in my pot.

"What are you making?" asks Guk.
"Stone stew," I say.
"Put in your carrots,
and I will share it with you."

"Okay," says Guk.
He puts the carrots
in my pot.

"What are you making?" asks Nug.
"Stone stew," I say.
"Put in your meat,
and I will share it with you."

"Okay," says Nug.
She puts the meat
in my pot.

Yay!
The stone stew is done.

I give some to Mub
and Guk and Nug.

Look!
There is some stone stew left.

I know what to do!
I make wheels.

I put them on a cart.

"Good-bye, Mub and Guk
and Nug," I say.
"Come to my cave
for more stone stew!"